The GINGERBREAD MAN

LOOSE at the ZOO

Laura Murray

illustrated by Mike Lowery

SCHOLASTIC INC.

To Lisa and Mark—my TGBS and TGBB!
I'm so grateful for your support, advice,
and encouragement through the years.
I'm lucky to be your TGLS!
-L.M.

For Allister and Katrin,
who make life pretty awesome.
—M.L.

ISBN 978-1-338-21759-9

12 11 10 9 8 7 6 5 4 3 2 1   17 18 19 20 21 22

Printed in the U.S.A.   40

First Scholastic printing, September 2017

Design by Ryan Thomann
Text set in Bokka and Dr. Eric, with a bit of hand-lettering
The illustrations were rendered with pencil, traditional screen printing, and digital color.

I woke to the sound of a rumbling
ROAR!
and
hooting,
and
howling,
and
growling
galore.

I ran to my window to see this strange creature.

GRRR!

Imagine my **shock** when I saw my own
TEACHER!

My **classmates** all giggled.
I joined in
their game.

HEE HEE   HA HA

"**HAVE A WILD DAY!**" said a man at the **front**
as we pulled **out** our **riddles** to start on the **hunt**.

RIDDLE #1

I'm spotted. I'm gentle.
I'm tall as a tree.
A branch full of leaves is
the best snack for me.
I have a new baby,
and she is my calf.

AH-HA!

we all shouted.

"THE ANSWER'S ...

We followed the signs as we raced down the trail,

till we spied her **long legs** and her **thin spotted tail.**

I jumped
on the railing
to get a
good **look,**

and **out** popped her **tongue**
like a curvy blue **hook.**

She **SCOOPED** me up high as her tongue curled **around**, but nobody noticed below on the **ground**.

My **classmates** were busily reading clue **two**.

OH, NO,

I cried out.

SHE'S BEGINNING TO CHEW!

I tickled her nose and she let out a **sneeze**.

Then I **zoomed** through the air to some **tropical trees**.

A long, loopy **vine** twisted **down** and **around**.
So I whipped up my courage and **swung** to the **ground**.

I glanced at my paper, then knew what to do—

I heard a loud **rustle** and turned in **surprise** to a small cheeky **monkey** with curious eyes.

He picked at my **buttons**, then tried for my **hat**.

He stayed on my **tail** as I dodged through the **grass**, but I **squeezed** underneath the tall habitat **glass**.

I waved to the

ZEBRA,

THE RHINO,

THE **SEAL,** who was slurping down fish for her afternoon meal.

The crocodile opened his big

TOOTHY TRAP.

He eyed me like
I'd make a good ginger **SNAP!**

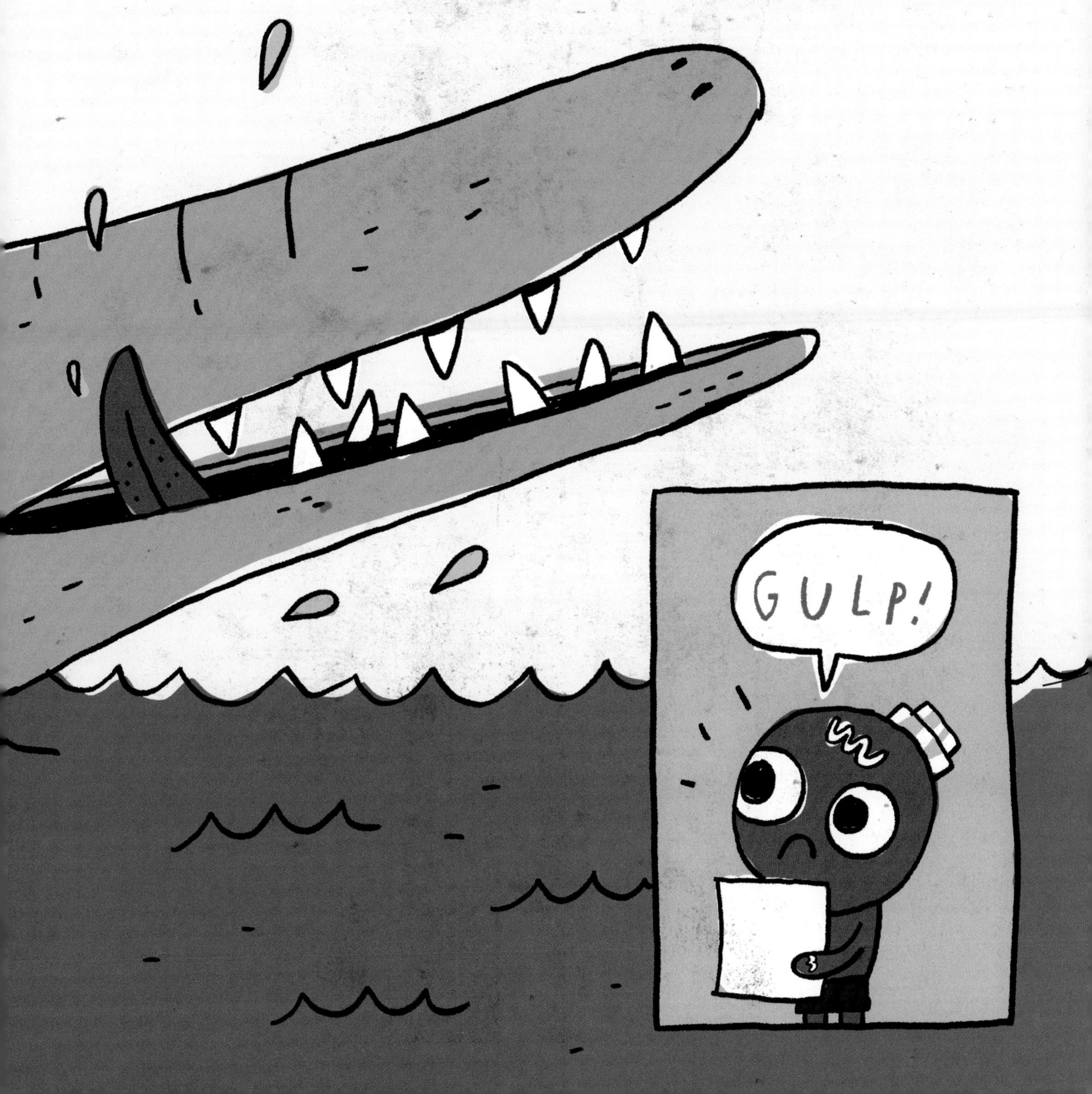

I raced down the path and my feet fairly **flew**.

Then **out** from a shrub popped a small **kangaroo**.

She started to **whimper**, hopped **this way** and **that**, then **snuffled**, and **shuffled**, and **slumped** as she **sat**.

ARE YOU **LOST**, LITTLE JOEY?
I'LL HELP YOU GET **BACK**.
I'M KIND OF LOST, TOO,
BUT I'M ON THE RIGHT **TRACK**.

She opened her **POCKET** and pointed **inside.** I **tucked** myself in and said,

We **hopped** down the path to the grassy **savanna** and **spied** a large crowd near the outback **cabana**.

I **popped** from her pocket and jumped to the **ground**.

She sprang to her mom with a long leaping **bound**.

My classmates all pointed and let out a cheer.

WE FOLLOWED THE RIDDLES AND FOUND YOU ALL HERE!

YOU'RE SUCH A SMART COOKIE! YOU HELPED SAVE THE DAY. OUR JOEY GOT LOST, AND YOU SHOWED HER THE WAY.

I'M SO VERY PROUD OF MY SUPER ZOO CREW! NOW IT'S TIME TO HEAD BACK TO OUR HABITAT, TOO.